LITTLE MISS NEAT
and the last leaf

Original concept by Roger Hargreaves
Illustrated and written by Adam Hargreaves

MR. MEN   LITTLE MISS

World International

Little Miss Neat likes things to be neat.

Which is why she is called Little Miss Neat.

She likes things to be as neat as two new pins.

Which is why her cottage is called Two Pin Cottage.

One Autumn day Miss Neat looked out of her window to admire her very neat garden.

As she looked, a leaf fell from the tree in the middle of her lawn.

"Oh goodness gracious!" she cried. "What a mess!"

She rushed outside, picked up the leaf, went back indoors and put the leaf in her rubbish bin.

"That's better," she said to herself.

But when she looked out of the window again there was another leaf lying on her immaculate lawn.

Out she rushed again and picked up the leaf and put it in the bin.

And so it went on all day long.

Rushing backwards and forwards until it was too dark to see anything.

Poor Little Miss Neat was exhausted.

"I don't like Autumn," she murmured to herself as she fell asleep.

The next morning was even worse.

Little Miss Neat had to sprint to keep up with the falling leaves.

And that was how Mr Happy found her at lunchtime.

Running backwards and forwards.

"You look exhausted," said Mr Happy.

"I am," puffed Miss Neat, "but I have to pick up all these horrid, messy leaves."

"Do you know what I do?" said Mr Happy. "I wait until all the leaves have fallen and then I pick them up. You ought to try it. It's much easier."

After Mr Happy had left, Miss Neat thought about what he had said and decided she would try it.

But it was easier said than done.

Poor Little Miss Neat worried and fretted and fretted and worried as the leaves slowly covered her lawn.

She hated it.

But eventually all the leaves had fallen.

Well, nearly all the leaves.

There was just one leaf left in the tree.

Little Miss Neat waited.

And waited.

And waited.

When it got too dark to see she got a torch and waited.

And waited.

And waited.

All night long!

And that was how Mr Happy found her the next morning.

Still waiting!

"What are you doing?" asked Mr Happy.

"What you suggested I should do," replied Miss Neat. "I'm waiting for all the leaves to fall."

Mr Happy smiled, reached up and plucked the last leaf from the tree.

"Oh," said Miss Neat suddenly feeling rather foolish.

And she blushed.

Mr Happy helped her to rake up all the leaves.

And by teatime Little Miss Neat's garden was as neat and as tidy as it usually was.

"You know what you should do next year?" said Mr Happy.

"Oh please! No more suggestions!" cried Miss Neat.

"Don't worry," said Mr Happy "You'll like this one. I think that next year you should go on holiday and ask Mr Busy to clear up the leaves. It wouldn't take him a minute."

"What a good idea!" said Miss Neat.

"You've taken a leaf out of my book," smiled Mr Happy.

"And turned over a new leaf," chuckled Miss Neat.

"You can leaf through the holiday brochures," giggled Mr Happy.

"And I can leave the leaves behind," laughed Miss Neat.

"Hee hee, oh stop it, hee hee hee," laughed Mr Happy.

"Leaf me alone! Ha! Ha! Ha!"

3 Great Offers For Mr Men Fans

1 FREE Door Hangers and Posters

In every Mr Men and Little Miss Book like this one you will find a special token. Collect 6 and we will send you either a brilliant Mr. Men or Little Miss poster and a Mr Men or Little Miss double sided, full colour, bedroom door hanger. Apply using the coupon overleaf, enclosing six tokens and a 50p coin for your choice of two items.

Egmont World tokens can be used towards any other Egmont World / World International token scheme promotions, in early learning and story / activity books.

Posters: Tick your preferred choice of either Mr Men ☐ or Little Miss ☐

Door Hangers: Choose from: Mr. Nosey & Mr Muddle ☐, Mr Greedy & Mr Lazy ☐, Mr Tickle & Mr Grumpy ☐, Mr Slow & Mr Busy ☐, Mr Messy & Mr Quiet ☐, Mr Perfect & Mr Forgetful ☐, Little Miss Fun & Little Miss Late ☐, Little Miss Helpful & Little Miss Tidy ☐, Little Miss Busy & Little Miss Brainy ☐, Little Miss Star & Little Miss Fun ☐. (Please tick)

2 Mr Men Library Boxes

Keep your growing collection of Mr Men and Little Miss books in these superb library boxes. With an integral carrying handle and stay-closed fastener, these full colour, plastic boxes are fantastic. They are just £5.49 each including postage. Order overleaf.

3 Join The Club

To join the fantastic Mr Men & Little Miss Club, check out the page overleaf NOW!

MR MEN and LITTLE MISS™ & © 1998 Mrs. Roger Hargreaves

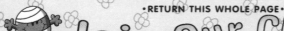

Join Our Club!

MR.MEN & little miss CLUB

When you become a member of the fantastic Mr Men and Little Miss Club you'll receive a personal letter from Mr Happy and Little Miss Giggles, a club badge with your name, and a superb Welcome Pack (pictured below right).

You'll also get birthday and Christmas cards from the Mr Men and Little Misses, 2 newsletters crammed with special offers, privileges and news, and a copy of the 12 page Mr Men catalogue which includes great party ideas.

If it were on sale in the shops, the Welcome Pack alone might cost around £13. But a year's membership is just £9.99 (plus 73p postage) with a 14 day money-back guarantee if you are not delighted!

HOW TO APPLY To apply for any of these three great offers, ask an adult to complete the coupon below and send it with appropriate payment and tokens (where required) to: Mr Men Offers, PO Box 7, Manchester M19 2HD. Credit card orders for Club membership ONLY by telephone, please call: 01403 242727.

To be completed by an adult

❏ **1.** Please send a poster and door hanger as selected overleaf. I enclose six tokens and a 50p coin for post (coin not required if you are also taking up 2. or 3. below).

❏ **2.** Please send ___ Mr Men Library case(s) and ___ Little Miss Library case(s) at £5.49 each.

❏ **3.** Please enrol the following in the Mr Men & Little Miss Club at £10.72 (inc postage)

Fan's Name:_____Fan's Address:_____

_____Post Code:_____Date of birth:___/___/___

Your Name:_____Your Address:_____

Post Code:_____Name of parent or guardian (if not you):_____

Total amount due: £_____ (£5.49 per Library Case, £10.72 per Club membership)

❏ I enclose a cheque or postal order payable to Egmont World Limited.

❏ Please charge my MasterCard / Visa account.

Card number: | | | | | | | | | | | | | | | | | |

Expiry Date: ____/____   Signature: _____

Data Protection Act: If you do **not** wish to receive other family offers from us or companies we recommend, please tick this box ❏. Offer applies to UK only